Love Notes
scribbled on my iphone

Poetry
by Sol Smith

for Sue

Write Something Beautiful

I used to stay up late
Writing in a yellow clearing
Of lamplight.
Or sit alone among the other
Poets and novelists in
Classrooms or cafes.

All that time, it turns out,
Was a youthful attribute.
Writing now is a between activity,
Before or after something else
That is cut a little short.

And it's not that I've given up,
So much as taken more on,
Staying up late with her,
Transmuting alone into together and
Together into everything.

And with her lips,
With her eyes,
Her fingers,
And the very tides of her body,
She urges me:
"Write something beautiful."

Fresno, California

Fresno, in the summer, is
shot on overexposed film,
the world washed in light,
squinting behind sunglasses.

Let's dig beneath the heat,
past the soil and hardpan,
and plant a garden in the
cool air underneath.

Let's carve the walls of clay
and let the ceiling hang with
grapes and oranges and lemons,
and the light down here will
filter and soften through round openings.

We can light a candle
and turn on a record, which will
reverberate in the hallways,
and let the people above walk
past in various hurries,
breathing carbon through open
mouths, while we discover
the secrets that the earth underfoot
holds dear in each other's eyes.

In Your Sway

We have a word for when we miss someone.
For homesickness.
For regret.
But what is the opposite?
What is the word that says,
"I am wrapped in you,
I'm not going away,
We are home when we are together."?

Where is the language to express
 a longing you've already sated?
Gravity is a small matter. When
I lift a fork, I defeat the pull of
an entire planet smug with life
and written history.
The pull of a kiss you're in the act of
kissing distorts spacetime,
making fabric of your feelings and
stretching it taught.

The jet stream confluence of
our bodies deserves a word that
counters the feeling of longing,
by magnifying the necessity of what
we already have.

Don't say, *Oh, you mean Love?*
Don't talk to me of that teenager's
word of lips and flowers and raised eyebrows.
I'm talking about oxygen relief in
submerged lungs.
I'm talking about waking up from a
continual nightmare.
Not pretty things that tickle and delight,
but massive forces that pull and consume
in much more than flames.
Don't prod at me with your assumptions
that my feelings boil down to a word
overused and oversold,
a coin for understanding that has been minted
a thousand times more than a penny.

Love is part of it, fine, but so is the sky
at night and the draw of an absent
Center where once all matter stood,
the background radiation of all being
remembering when it once belonged
and being the only two in accord.
There should be a word for that.

Soft Glass

An early light is woven
By the sound of waves.
Bare footprints lapidate
Wet sand, erased, repeated.

Alone, bent down,
She examines a handful
Of sand, rescuing soft glass
From a dark forever.

The shapes her body makes
Against the lightening sky
Last as long as the feet
Lost in the sand.

A Perfect Night

It's cold and clear and covered
with stars.
It's a perfect night
to go to the beach and wish
we brought heavier sweaters.

But that's not all we could do,
because it's a perfect night
for staying in and dimming the lights
and our senses.
A perfect night
for washing our hair and folding
clothes and running hot water
over our skin and
performing other little acts of
self care.

It's a perfect night to tap
out patterns in the air in low voices
and share time and touches
and retell stories that need
repetition to become more real.

It's a perfect night to breathe
and sleep
and roll over in sync
and pretend

we can afford our rent
and that our future will be brighter
than our past beyond statistical
error.

And to forget the bruises we've
been dealt anyway
and smash open the reasons
we've conformed the ways we
have conformed and
to build and build
our little life
before we race each
other to old age and death and
everything else.

After all, it's cold
and clear
and covered
with stars.

Amarillo, Texas

A hotel parking lot,
lined by a low wood fence.
A sharp wind brings
the thick smell of horses.
No sounds, that night.

This is a distant memory,
stepping on the scrubby grass
that surrounded the asphalt,
looking up at the moon.

And I loved you even back then.

Soap

The wallpaper in this little alcove
Is pink, with carefully arranged flowers,
Creating lines going from the ceiling,
Past the counter, to the floor.

The sink warms up fast,
I'm thankful.
I note the light-purple shade of the
Soap before I place the smell.

Two obvious thoughts hit me:
The soap is lavender.
My father is dead, and
The soap is lavender.

Three Senryū About Love

It's not that she's sad
Because that would be better.
She can't feel anything.

"I don't care if I die,"
She calls down the darkness and
Cloisters in despair.

My light won't tarnish.
Don't change. Don't even feel better.
I will still love you.

Dinkey Creek

When you stand on a rock
In the middle of Dinkey Creek,
Your voice rides the rushing water,
Joining the tumult,
Projected by a hundred copacetic
Polished stones,
Ushered by the hallway of
Towering pines,
Speaking easily to an audience
A hundred yards downstream.

The audience in my mind as I write
Is my dad
And my golden retriever,
Both of whom loved the Creek
In a way that only those perfectly
At ease with the world they inhabit
Love a natural scene, as if
It sprang forth from their serenity.

Stepping off a rock,
The ice cold hurried water
Devours you fully.
How is it, my kids wonder, that I
Can hop right in this freshly melted snow,
When I avoid pools in May

And sometimes late June?

They can't understand how
I want to be held by the peace
And comfort that embraced my dog and
My dad,
As my staccato yelp
Rides the water easily
One hundred yards away.

Reading a Book of Poems by Mary Oliver

If I'm being completely honest,
I want to copy her.
But I shy away from honesty,
Repelled from the thought of
Being nothing
But a filter of better ideas
And expressions.

So I refine this.
I want my words to shake
With sympathetic vibrations,
Ringing back chords that
She struck
On her typewriter,
However long ago,
Sitting in a room lit by
A square of natural light
Falling on her shoulders like
A nostalgic rain.

And I go, "There. An image."
But, if I switch back to that pesky honesty
I feel like I barely managed
To filter what someone better might have thought,

If they felt the same way I do
About Mary Oliver.

We Are Lucky

We are lucky we like the stars,
since they are doomed to pierce
the darkness for billions of years.
Though some of those stars are gone,
while their candlelight flickers
through time and space, we can enjoy
what they once were without heartbreak.

We're lucky we like traveling.
We never rush to arrive
because we aren't looking for somewhere,
but simply search everywhere.

We're lucky we have each other,
because the collective efforts of all Time
have led to this moment,
and gravity put us together, bound by
things greater than ourselves,
even though it felt like a choice.

And someday one of us will be left
alone.
Whichever it is will feel the loss like
pain that will be the inverse of all
the contentment and bliss

that we have built.

But this is now.
I hold your hand.
Life need not be perfect
to be perfect.

This is 40

"We have no business
being 40," my wife says,
standing at the cusp of the age.
"We were just ten."

This piercing reality, so clearly stated,
wakes up my blood
and opens a hundred calculations.
I'm 40, and it hardly feels possible.
It's not just me who has gotten older,
the entire planet was 40 years younger
when I was born.

Every plant, every mountain, every
ancient drop of water
has grown older, too,
and held my hand on their
endless journey.

Forty years is a blink between
inches of circle
for the trees.
When the they saw me take my first steps,
they smiled at the passing clouds,
proud to see the progress.
When I learned to swim, the water
sent warm feelings to the stones.

My wedding was attended by
a herd of grasses, aloof birds and stoic
carbons, all holding back tears to see
me so grown-up.
The gap between my birth
and my daughters'
was a breath for the redwoods,
and I can feel their grandmother
gazes when we gather below their canopy.

We camp, and the dry logs release
the sunlight that their mother trees
gathered over their years,
surrendering their partnership in our
aging.

"Forty will be great,"
they whisper through flames.
"We've been there,
we know."

First Time

I'm going to throw this out there
and I want you to know that I don't
especially expect you
to understand,
and that's not because you're
dumb or unsympathetic or anything,
but because I am going to veer away
from not just common poetic sentiment,
but common culture, as well.

It takes me a moment to remember
the color of your eyes.
I know the name, but I mean
how they look.
Even worse, I have to think very hard
to conjure up the color of your hair.
Or the length.

You have that one tooth
that's out of place,
so if I start there I can get your smile
in focus, and then your face.
There are your eyes, now,
but just the shape, not the color.

I've always thought it's strange
that we think it's so important
how the light jumps off of our forms,
how it makes us feel.
How people will die
or spend their lives on
how someone else looks
But I have to admit that I'm addicted
to the endorphin rush I feel when
I see your shirt strain against you.

I have trouble picturing you,
but every time I see your face,
I see it new,
I see it for the first time
again.

The Moon is Full Behind the Clouds

The cold rain is coming down
in sheets,
and maybe that's why the kids
are crawling the walls.
The dog, of course, would be
climbing them anyway.

Birds are nesting somewhere,
no doubt,
and deep under the sea, squid
are hiding, and whales are sleeping,
hanging in the water like celestial bodies.

But not here.

Here, the volume is up
and girls (both teen and preteen)
are claiming opposing positions
regardless of what they think or feel,
because conflict has its own reward
to their boiling blood.

And the dog must get something
out of closing

his teeth around the skin
of the humans he loves.

Somewhere, a mother alligator
soothes her eggs with deep, guttural
vibrations. Somewhere a night
guard hears her footsteps
echo through an empty cathedral.
In the Kepler Belt, there are grooves
of rock filled with loneliness
and darkness
and they've never heard a sound.

But here the gates of growth
have opened wide and they fount
energy through the fiery
pores of my daughters, manifesting
in bloodthirsty sparring matches
and the dog has found new objects
to devour
all because the cold rain runs down the window and,
presumably,
the moon is full behind the clouds.

Gallup, New Mexico

Behind a wall of sculpted rock,
an unimpressive town is huddled
along Interstate 40 and a train track.
They used to film westerns near here
and their vintage hotel has
pictures to prove it.

A long stretch of road,
that must be old Route 66,
houses a collection of turquoise
that requires discretion to
illuminate.

Okay.
Let me stop right there.
I need to shift gears
and to be honest, I'm sitting
here writing about Gallup,
and as hard as I try,
I'm not thinking about
the town at all. Listen:

Outside of town,
over 20 years ago,
I watched four people die.

It took hours
and there was nothing
any of us
could do
to stop
them.

And while it was gruesome
and I was succumb to a logjam
of feelings,
I was mostly relieved
that it wasn't me
as I had, just moments before,
driven between their two cars
as they bounced off each other.

A tremendous flash of energy
was followed by a plume of smoke
and the steel tore at their bodies
and the forces momentum
suddenly changing trajectory
pummeled them beyond reason.
We stood and talked and watched
them leave.

One by one.

Each dying of a totally different
disruption to their bodies.
Bones, blood, and
last-moment thoughts
on display.

I wonder who they were.

I see their faces all the time,
and I have no idea what
they were like before they
started dying
in their cars
one hot morning
outside of Gallup, New Mexico.

Quantum Love Song

If what we see and what we live
is the average of all realities,
the cozy midpoint if possible variation,

I'm glad for the way it all
balanced out.

I realize, by the definition, that
most of our realities were much like

our average; our various lives
are peppered by nearly indistinguishable
versions of our story.

We kiss just like this, but in some lives
a fiber or two of someone's scarf
rests slightly out of place;
or a worm is missing, deep below ground;
or the dust went *that* way through the air;
or I stubbed my toe once when I was twelve.

But there are also outliers,
lives of ours deep on the edges of the
multiverse where I am glad to average out:
We were never born; we are toads;

we are effervescent;
we only ride unicycles;
we burst into flames when
we use the letter "d" at the end of every sentence.

Every possibility is exhausted
out there somewhere:
We kiss with our hands; we kiss with
our eyebrows; we do not kiss at all;
or, we never met; or our magnified
love ends the world in a burst
of deadly passion.

When all the realities are weighed,
we've met and we're here
and I've written this tiny verse on my
electric hand-screen and things can't be
very bad.
In this maze of probabilities
if our average is so good.

Warming Light

Outside the tent,
there's a bird who seems to be
in some kind of panic,
but only when I start to drift off.

The coals are still hot
enough to kindle flame
to a morning log
and the fire is hot enough
to make coffee.

The coffee doesn't ward
off the panicking bird,
but her voice doesn't bother
those left in the tent.

It's easier to breathe in
the warming mountain light.
It's easier to be awake,
with a book
and coffee.
The bird was panicked
that I would sleep through
this realization.

Failing Light

Art that takes place in time
is called music.
Improving on silence
is a monumental accomplishment.

In the noise of our lives,
most settle for an organization
of sound that cuts through
the chaotic miasma.

The tape player on my dad's desk
turned its wheels and played
a music that grew out of surrounding
quiet.

It was the same with his words:
An improvement of silence.

Crystalline Growth

The molecular shape of
a bead of water
gives snowflakes their six-fold
symmetry.

What signature
between us has shaped
our space in the world?

In which strand of information
did you lie locked within me,
waiting for us to meet?

When you spoke in a dark, empty
room, did you hear my voice
in the echo?

What happens when we melt?

Ballet Class

The children learn to make shapes
out of their bodies,
while parents grab clips of
the acrobatics through the window.

The piano sounds puncture the air
through full throated speakers,
no Baby Grand to make the floors
vibrate in sympathy.

The parents, eyes on phones,
phones on children,
sometimes wonder why their backs ache.
Did they abandon their bodies,
or did their bodies abandon them?

What would it feel like to be a kid again,
the world barely pulling at you?
If we could do it again, would
we leap in the air and never come down?

Arrow of Time

Sunlight and carbon build
boughs and bark anchored
in the ground.

Sometime, hundreds of years before,
the bent wood of a violin
was already inside the tree,
even when the tree was already inside
the seed.

If all things could grow
and change
and die
and be harvested in such
enriching ways, then entropy
would be a tangled growth of
music and passion and love, instead
of the steep inclined walkway
to heartbreak.

Laguna Beach, California

The way the light slips
on the surface tension of the water
lets you notice something from
this angle that you've known
without knowing;
that the ocean hangs on the planet
like a globular bubble.

You also know that the palms aren't trees,
but a species of grass.
Your senses tell you something else:
a palm is an natural obelisk,
pointing your eyes toward the sun.

The aloes bloom—tremendous and pink.
They reach up, spread out—
mandalas that drink water.

Now I'll stop—you deserve my silence,
so you can hear it all.

We Should Dance

We should dance.
We should grab each other's bodies
and make synchronized movements
across an open floor
while musicians make the air shake.

We should work backbreaking jobs
and cool ourselves off in the shade
with ladles of water, sighing
at the work and the sweat and the hole
that we need to fill with each other
at the end of the day.

Cleaning up after working outside
should be a time-consuming ritual,
our muscles aching in satisfaction,
looking forward to eating,
and laughing after a long day of restraint.

The mirrors we look in while we dress
should be tall and kind of foggy
and the bones of our old house should
creak when we walk downstairs in
nicer shoes than the ones we used to
climb them.

The car should start right away,
but it won't, and we will wonder
if the whole night is a wash,
and therefore the day, and
we will curse it and it will start and
we will feel the relief all over again.

Inside, we will eat food that we
did not cook
and the music will play
and our arms and legs will be loose
from the work and the sun and the
heat and our hearts will want to let loose
from the restraint, the halter of
putting together a life and a living.

And the right song will be played,
and then we should dance.

Between the Ranges

The children of the valley
know the taste of dust in their throats
and remember when the horizon
was saturated with orchards.

The children of the valley
rejoice in the rain and snap pictures
of the wet, reflective skies
in the aftermath of celebration.
Handed down from farm owner
or fieldworker or both
a terrific conversational vernacular
abounds around the weather

The children of the valley
know enough to feel left out
by the bigger cities that taunt them
and know enough to stay away
from constant busy droning lives
that they help feed
and help them fear
gear-working outsiders.

The children of the valley
play on surrounding hillsides

swim in distant waters,
shedding drought-tolerant natures
in the immersion of brighter air.

43

Elgin, Texas

Our kids were too young
to remember napping in the graveyard.
But it's stuck with us,
that near-daily ritual, hiding in
the shade after driving aimlessly
just to get the babies to sleep.

They don't remember the waitress
who loved to carry them around,
letting us eat in peace.
And my god, they don't remember
the food. But we do.

They're lucky not to remember
the money problems
or the sleep deprivation
or the postpartum depression
or the endless press for survival.

Things have gotten better
since then.
But even our lives there, at that time,
would have been enough.

Migration

The wind brought panic
in the form of orange butterflies.
Hundreds of folded flowers slipping
on the current.

Pointing and jumping,
my daughters hoped
they would land
like bows in their hair.

"Next year," one of the girls said,
"we will see them again. But
then it will be their great-granddaughters."

It seems unique to butterflies
that they don't make it home.
But next year, we are always
our own children.

Shortcuts

What if instead is using pictures,
we had to use those thousand words
to express this moment or that?

What if we had to spoon our feelings
to each other, instead of relying upon
well-trodden words?

What if our memories eased and we got
to see each other's faces each time
new, over and over?

Our necessary shortcuts, that make
regular life possible
should sometimes let us live impossibly.

Meditation

Quiet sounds disturb
the cultivated silence.
Focus, breathe, repeat.

Turquoise

Today the ocean was
a ridiculous shade of turquoise.
It's amazing how effective
a color of water can be
at drowning out the spectrum
of reality that deals with
stress and money and deadlines
and danger and suffering
and hunger and inequality
and every other struggle
I will and will not know
just for the moment it takes for
the placid, turquoise water
to swell into violence
on the shore.

School Pick Up

Springtime, Southern California.
I'm sitting in my car
having arrived a little early,
just so I could close my eyes,
and the wind brings in the smell
of some remarkable flower.

It stirs a memory of somewhere
I've never been;
someplace tropical with wandering
pathways on top of adobe walls
connecting rooms both
outdoor and in.

I like the smell, but those flowers
have left me
in loss of something
I've never had.

Mid-April

She does to my blood
what jasmine does to the air
and you can hear the star blossoms
erupt in my breath.

Bonfire

Wind whips the flames
of a bonfire on the beach,
making the heat at once necessary
and intolerable.
Cold sand grinds out
deep footprints and
sings through the salt-kissed air.
The light casts shadows
on the stars.

We should have brought only
blankets and chairs
to huddle against the cold
and listen to wave breaks while
the sky buds in outer space
ornamentation,
the cold of the empty sky
reaching down, but unable to
penetrate our collective solitude,
glowing like embers.

Stopping the world takes quiet
and stillness in all things but
our hearts.

Equinox

Early clouds clear
to free the first spring moon,
Forcing poetry from amateurs.

Black Hills, South Dakota

We were lying on our backs
looking up at the stars framed
by the sky-reaching pines
that grew all over the Black Hills.

This was the final leg of our honeymoon
and we were broke
and we had no idea where
we would live in a few weeks
but we had a good tent.

Lying there, whispering, holding hands
we felt sorry for literally every other
thing in all of Creation.

I Had a Poem

I had a poem written the other day
and all that was left to do was just a little typing.
I'm sitting here now just wondering
how it went.
There was a cascade of words that lilted
out a lovely thought,
though I can't remember which one.

Something about the two of
us and the lines
patterns of tree leaves,
or summer-warmed moonlight
on our skin,
something that brought to light
the wonderful, painful way
we've carved a universe for ourselves
out of the ones we were given.

I thought and thought about it
and then I fell asleep
or had to work
and here I am, wondering how it went.

About *Love Songs Scribbled on My iPhone*

I'm not really a poet, but I've always admired poets. Poets are people who stack their thoughts in certain ways and see things in certain ways, and try and capture the negative space of things while trying to connect their emotion with that of another. Maybe I'm wrong about that, and if I am, I shouldn't have to pay any student loan money back, and if I'm right, I'd rather not pay, either. But in both cases, I think that what I'm saying is that language is not sufficient, always, in conveying feeling, and we all feel that plenty.

We can woo and swish our words around like poets all we want, but to think like one takes a) reading, and b) practice, and probably other letters, too. I've been reading poetry for a long while and practice and discipline come to me in short periods of intensity. Once it gets going, and one of my kids can detect in me the makings of a makeshift poet; I will see an interesting tree shadow while sitting at a red light and they will roll their eyes with words, "Great, this is going to be a poem."

Honestly, it's their fault for following my writing account on Instagram.

Fiction doesn't take as much discipline or as much faith. Creative nonfiction takes a commitment to honesty, but still not as much in the way of reengineering the brain. This is my experience, not yours, so if you disagree you should write a poem about it. But this book is the result of a few months of discipline, faith in my ability to see past my imperfections and maintain a powerful ego despite vulnerability, and a willingness to offer my poems to the world for as cheaply as possible, hoping not to insult my poet friends or embarrass my family.

Last, of course, poetry is painting with emotion, and that primary emotion is found in my love for my wife. Her endless tolerance of my pretentiousness allows my verbal experimentation in a public forum. I love you, Sue, and it's probably worth searching the Notes app on my iPhone if I die tragically, in case there are more little love notes to you mixed in with the shopping lists, interesting quotes, and quantum pondering.

www.ingramcontent.com/pod-product-compliance
Lightning Source LLC
Chambersburg PA
CBHW020938160726
47993CB00007B/2838